A huge thank-you to my friends
Sylvie Kantorovitz and Barbara Lehman

Who Needs a Bath?
Copyright © 2015 by Jeff Mack
All rights reserved. Manufactured in China.
No part of this book may be used or reproduced in any manner whatsoever without written permission except
in the case of brief quotations embodied in critical articles and reviews. For information address HarperCollins
Children's Books, a division of HarperCollins Publishers, 195 Broadway, New York, NY 10007.
www.harpercollinschildrens.com

ISBN 978-0-06-222028-8 (trade bdg.)

The artist used ink and pencil on paper and Photoshop to create the digital illustrations for this book.
Typography by Dana Fritts
15 16 17 18 19   SCP   10 9 8 7 6 5 4 3 2 1
❖
First Edition

Who Needs a Bath?

Written and illustrated by
JEFF MACK

HARPER
An Imprint of HarperCollinsPublishers

It was Skunk's birthday.
Bear had a plan.

PARTY AT THE POND!
DON'T TELL SKUNK.
IT'S A SURPRISE!

There was just one problem:

Who wants to party with a stinky skunk?

Not me!

PU!

PARTY AT THE
DON'T TELL
IT'S A SURP

Even Bear had
to admit it:

**SKUNK
STUNK!**

PAINT

Bear had an idea.

"Hello, Skunk. How would you like to take a bath?"

"Ha!" said Skunk. "Why would I want that?"

"Because baths are fun," said Bear. "They make you smell nice!"

"Well, I'm a skunk, see? And skunks never take baths!"

Luckily, Bear had another idea.

"This slide will make your bath fun," he said.

"I doubt it," said Skunk.

"Just try it," said Bear. "You'll go really fast!"

"Okay," said Skunk. "But I'll need a push."

"One push coming up," said Bear.

"Push harder!"
said Skunk.

"I am pushing harder!" said Bear.

Ha! Ha!
Ha! Ha!

"Almost there!"

"See?" said Bear.
"This bath is fun!"

"You were right about the fast slide," said Skunk. "But that bath does *not* look like fun!"

Luckily, Bear had *another* idea.
"This swing will make your
bath fun," he said.

"You'll feel like you're flying!"

"Okay," said Skunk. "But only
if we can swing together."

"Hop on!"
said Bear.

"There. Now doesn't this bath
look like fun?" asked Bear.

"You were right about flying," said Skunk,
"but that bath does *not* look like fun!"

BLOOP!

Luckily, Bear had *another* idea.

"It's a trampoline," said Bear.
"Now you can bounce into your bath."

"That's not fun,"
said Skunk.

"It is if you bounce
high," said Bear.

BOING!

"BOING!"

"BOING!"

"You call that high?" asked Skunk.

"How about this?" said Bear.

"BOING!"

"Higher!" cried Skunk. "Bounce higher!"

Ha! Ha! Ha! Ha!

"Oops," said Bear.

"That's too high," said Skunk.

"No, it's not," said Bear. "Can't you see how fun this is?"

"Okay," said Bear.
"Maybe it was too high.
But it was fun!"

"That bath does *not*
look like fun!" said Skunk.
"I'll never take a bath!"

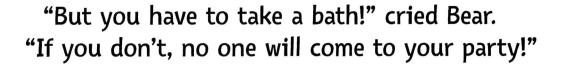

"But you have to take a bath!" cried Bear.
"If you don't, no one will come to your party!"

"Huh?" asked Skunk.
"What party?"

"Oops," said Bear.

Did someone
say party?

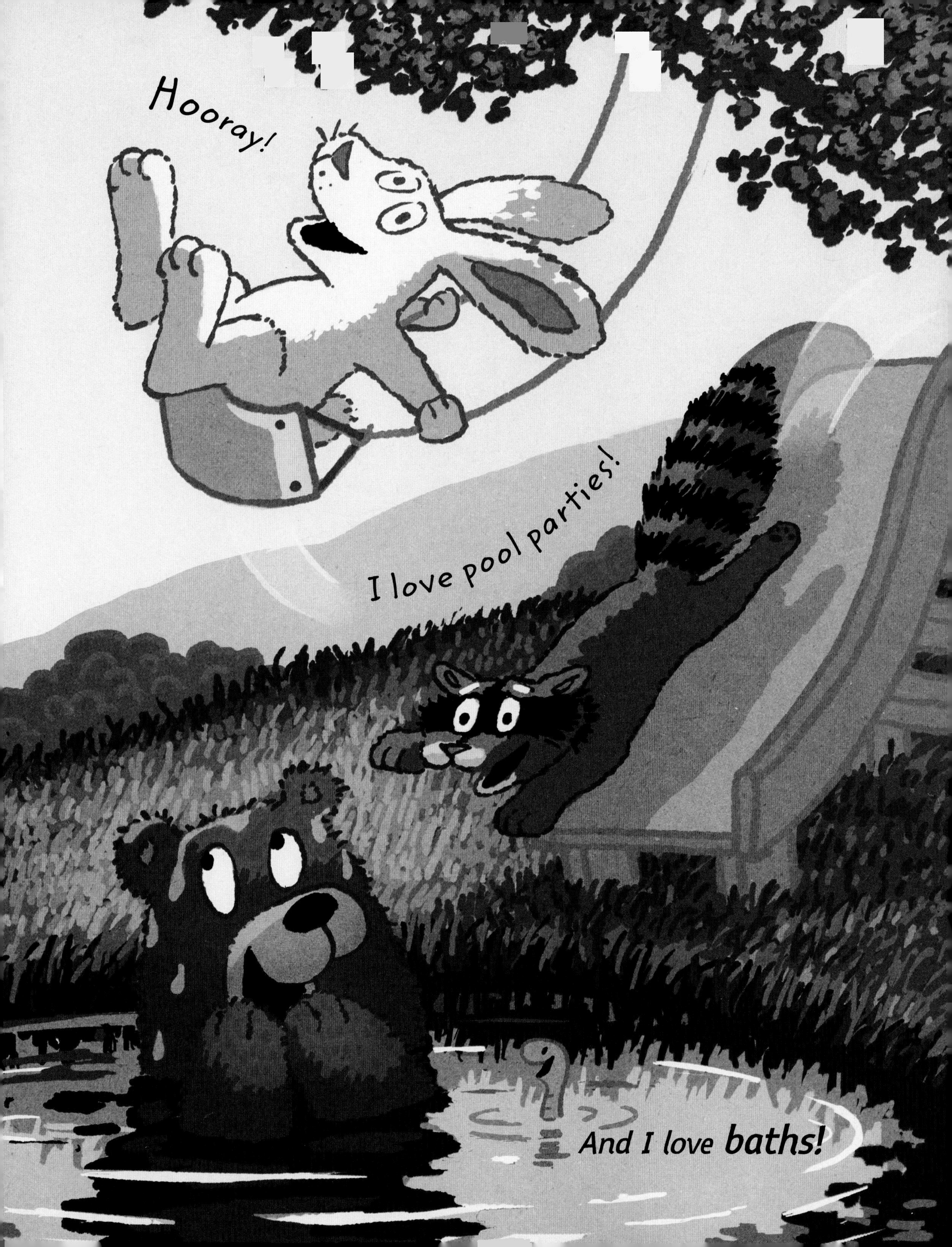
Hooray!
I love pool parties!
And I love baths!

"Wait!" cried Skunk. "What about me?!
I want to have fun too!

"It's *my* birthday!
Where's *my* surprise?"

SQUISH!

"Look out!" cried Bear.

"Oops!"

SOAP

SLIP!

"That . . .

. . . was . . .

. . . AWESOME!"

"I told you baths are fun," said Bear.

"You were right," said Skunk.

"What a surprise!"